Y0-AAZ-854

THE
COACHMAN
&
THE BELLS

A Christmas Story

THE
COACHMAN
&
THE BELLS

A Christmas Story

Ted C. Hindmarsh

Cover Art by Sam Richardson

Copyright © 1988
Horizon Publishers & Distributors, Inc.

All rights reserved. Reproduction in whole or any
parts thereof in any form or by any media without
written permission is prohibited.

ISBN: 0-88290-340-3

Horizon Publishers' Catalog and Order Number:
1973

First Printing, September 1988

Printing: 2   3   4   5   6   7   8   9   10

Printed and distributed
in the United States of America by

Horizon
Publishers
& Distributors, Incorporated
P.O. Box 490 Bountiful, Utah 84010-0490

Table of Contents

1. Joe Turner's Emptiness 9

2. The Coachman 15

3. Commitment 23

4. The Party................................... 28

5. Another View of Christmas.................... 31

6. The Gifts 37

7. The Checkered Coat......................... 42

8. The Christmas Eve Jail 46

9. The Bells 55

Epilogue 61

To Shirlene...

Who personifies the same wonderful attributes as the Coachman...

And who truly knows how to give herself away.

1. Joe Turner's Emptiness

"What in the samhill do you think this is? No! I absolutely will not give to your lousy charity! Christmas comes around and you guys use it as an annual excuse to rip off honest, hard working people! It's legalized, traditional robbery! I'm fed up with the likes of you and the way you take advantage of what is supposed to be a spiritual event to bilk your fellowman of his hard-earned cash! Now get out of here before I call building security and have you thrown out! And don't come back next year either!"

The volume that bellowed from the young executive permeated the outer office and seemed to shake the windows. The dozen employees who sat at their desks buried their eyes in their work and pretended not to notice the two strangers hurrying out the door nor the color of their boss's face. Its rage-reddened hue exaggerated his boyish brown-blond hair, and his blue eyes seemed to shoot fire as he yelled after the two hapless fund raisers.

A worried glance darted from the pretty secretary seated at the large oak reception desk to a small-framed plain looking woman with grayish hair tied up in a bun, who sat in a nearby chair awaiting her turn.

"I don't think this is the time to bring it up," the secretary whispered as their eyes met. The woman with the bun nodded her head ever so slightly and stood to try an unnoticed exit.

"Wait a minute, Mildred! Now where are you going?"

The sharp, chilled voice froze the older woman in place.

"What were you two whispering about? What's going on? I thought you wanted to see me!" it challenged.

To say that the woman visibly trembled may be an overstatement, but only a slight one.

"Well don't just stand there. I'm not going to bite." The voice was calming down, but only a little.

"Well...Mr. Turner," Mildred mumbled timidly, "Maybe I could ask later, when you're...." Oops. That was not what she should have said, and she knew it instantly.

"When I'm what? When I've simmered down a little? I know, I know. I'm OK now. I can handle it. Well, go ahead. Ask, woman! Ask anything you want, as long as it isn't something stupid, like will I put on that ridiculous red get-up I saw hanging in the coat closet and play Santa Claus at the Christmas party tonight!"

Mildred looked like someone had just pulled the plug that held all her color in place. She turned rigidly and gazed with a look of horrified amazement at the perplexed secretary. Someone at one of the desks near the back of the room stifled a giggle. Mildred sunk back into the chair and stared at the opposite wall in disbelief.

"Come on now, Mildred! Was that really it?" Again the face of the young boss reddened, and his fiery eyes danced around the room. Suddenly everyone was very busy.

"You turkeys, all of you! Whose side are you on anyway?" The voice had nearly reached full volume again.

"If you think I'm going to put that moth-eaten outfit on and act like a buffoon, you're all nuts! Christmas makes people absolutely crazy. I'm Santa Claus enough to all of you for the rest of the year, and don't any of you forget it!"

The door slammed as he stomped back into his office. Everyone looked shell-shocked. A few eyebrows raised, but no one spoke.

Mildred was still white and seated where she had sunk when, after several tense minutes, the door slowly opened again. The youthful boss, now much subdued, came quietly out.

"I'm sorry everyone. I really am," he said softly. "Mildred, I apologize. For some reason I get this way at Christmas time.

I don't mean to, and it's not your fault, any of you. You're all wonderful. And it wasn't the fault of those fellows who were here with their hands out either. They were just trying to do their job."

A lot of eyes glanced to the floor. Some looked out the window.

"Something's not right in my heart. I just can't seem to get into Christmas gear like everyone else seems to. And as long as it isn't, I can't pretend to be Santa's helper or anything else I don't honestly feel."

His voice trailed off into the same distance that seemed to absorb his gaze. He went to the closet and took out his gloves and warm overcoat. With a certain preoccupation he turned to the secretary, whose pretty features were now saddened with empathy.

"I'm going to take a walk for lunch, Susan," he said quietly. "Will you cover for me? I'll be back in a while."

For Joe Turner, this sudden public display of repentance was totally uncharacteristic, and no one had ever known him to take a walk for lunch. He usually worked straight through with just a tuna sandwich and a caffeine-free cola. It was obvious to those who knew him that some powerful forces were at work inside him. His disenchantment was real. He felt some genuine uneasiness about the state of his heart, in fact, the state of his life.

The pretty secretary fought back an urgent feeling to grab her own coat and follow him, but a second thought held her back. Maybe it was better for him to be alone for awhile. In her heart it wasn't just a matter of Christmas charity that caused her concern. It had already become obvious to others that her feelings for him ran deeper than the surface of their professional relationship. She held an inward hope and belief that, if he could ever get around his blasted self-serving ego, some day even he would notice that she really cared for him.

As Joe meandered aimlessly through the busy holiday traffic his mind wrestled with his inner self. He had almost everything he had ever dreamed of. He had worked for it, he had earned it, and he was proud of it. He had a successful business, and he was still young and relatively happy. He hadn't married yet, however, and he was forced to admit occasionally that it troubled him. But, so far, there had never been room in his heart for anything but hard-nosed business dealings and a dominant drive to succeed in the demanding world of competition.

Joe had many associates, but there were only two that he could honestly call friends, and that was more because of their initiative than his. First there was Susan, who he freely admitted was a far better secretary, and much more devoted to him, than he deserved. If he ever did marry, he knew that he would never settle for anyone less than her. But how could he ever hope to saddle anyone so unselfish and genuine with an egotistical burden like him? For reasons he had never been able to figure out she was patient, caring, and, perhaps above all, she was willing to put up with his eccentricities. He knew that if he could learn to be more like her he would be much better off.

And then there was Charlie, his very able but sort of off-the-wall attorney. They had gone to school together, and their relationship went far beyond the routine legal work that was necessary for the operation of a thriving business. Charlie had always been a little weird. He liked unusual things, and was a big patsy for the under-dog. Though Joe had never thought much about it, that had to be the main reason Charlie was so willing to hang around.

Thank goodness for Sue and Charlie. They were socially smooth, and they kept Joe in touch, so to speak, with the human family. In fact, without them and the bash they had put together with the office crew for tonight, he would probably just spend a melancholy Christmas Eve alone by his fireplace.

But why? With everything else so reasonably good, why did he feel this confounded emptiness? That question had taken possession of his heart as well as his mind. It was becoming an obsession, and the joviality of Christmastime which surrounded him didn't help his mood a bit.

Christmas had never been Joe's favorite time of year. He wasn't personally religious or sentimental by nature. He was too practical, he thought. But neither did he appreciate what he called the "outrageous commercialism" of something that was obviously very special to a lot of other people and ought to be kept more sacred, for their sake if for nothing else, and he reasoned that for a red-blooded businessman that was quite a concession.

Joe knew that he wasn't recognized for his generosity, although he didn't feel that he was exactly stingy either. It was just a matter of professional horsesense. At least that was what he repeatedly told himself. He gave often, and he thought quite abundantly. For example, he'd made a substantial pledge to the high school band car wash. So what if he had the franchise on band uniforms? All his "gifts" were shrewdly placed where they were likely to "do the most good." But that was just sound business practice, right? That's how businesses operate.

But *something* wasn't right, and Joe wasn't stupid. Deep down, when he uncomfortably faced the issue, he suspected that his emptiness was because he was a loner. As successful as he had been at business, he had never been a hit with people. Sure, he had made well-calculated contributions to carefully selected charities, but he had never really learned how to give any part of his well-protected self.

He couldn't handle close personal relationships where something personal had to be risked. He was often heard to say that the hard, cold business world had taught him that people couldn't be trusted; the only one he could really count on was himself. That was why he had never been able to find a suitable business partner, although everyone knew he desperately needed one. The details of his demanding business were getting to him.

He was beginning to forget and leave important things undone. Even in his youth, weariness was settling in.

Inept as he was in the people business, Joe was smart enough to know that developing a trust relationship with another person meant giving of self, and that was the most difficult thing he ever had to do. That singular weakness was what made Christmases so difficult. He wanted to change, but how could he ignore a lifetime of cautious experience? Facts were facts. If he changed his time-proven formula, he reasoned, he would surely "loose his shirt" in this "unforgiving dog-eat-dog world."

Joe considered himself to be quite gentle normally, but he also took pride in his intensity. He was a survivor! Life in the big city jungle had taught him to be tough. Getting and keeping success in this crazy world took "guts" and "savvy." He had struggled and he had triumphed; even if it was at the sacrifice of those sensitive, personal elements that most men take for granted.

The more Joe walked and pondered, the more he tried to convince himself that he was really not that bad off. So he felt some uneasiness. Nobody could have everything. After all, he was *making* it, and he was proud of it. He had done it all on his own so far, and if that's the way it had to be, then that's just how it would have to be!

But then, from way down deep in a part of his heart that refused to be penetrated by all that worldly reasoning, a realization forced its way to the surface that if he was ever to be truly happy in this life, something basic was going to have to change. He was willing. Oh my, was he ever willing; if someway, he could only get a handle on that emptiness. He *had* to get a handle on it. He hadn't let it trouble him before, but he wasn't getting any younger. He had to find a way to erase that terrible alienation from humanity before it consumed him.

2. The Coachman

"There has to be a way," Joe mused aloud as he aimlessly wandered more than strolled. He'd already been away for over an hour, and he still didn't feel any great urgency to get back to the office. He cringed at the memory of his enraged outburst. He envied all those people back there who were so secure in their ego positions. They were supposed to look up to him as their fearless leader. Now they probably looked down on him with pity. Not me, he shuddered. Envy he could handle; or even hate. He was used to people staring at him with those emotions; but pity? No way! That was unthinkable.

Joe gradually abandoned the search for reason for the uncharacteristic thoughts he was thinking, for the extended mid-day break he was taking, or even for his choice of this particular route through the park. For now, he just wanted to kick back. He wasn't loosing his grip, he told himself. This was just a strategic retreat to regroup for the awesome charge he was about to muster. He sat down on a bench to watch the holiday bustle, which was another thing he just never did!

All of the park's pedestrians seemed jovial and caught up in the spirit of the season. Each person he saw seemed to have a firm grip on who she or he was, and an assurance of his or her individual destination. They seemed to smile easily as their glances met his while they bustled about, wrestling packages and puffing breaths of white vapor into the chilled December air. As a matter of fact, it was icy, even at 1:30 in the afternoon. Yet there was something stimulating about the way Joe's face and ears tingled, while the rest of him was warm and comfortable in his heavy overcoat and gloves.

Suddenly, one of Joe's glances caught a startling sight. He turned his head in the direction of the amusement. He watched with a magnetic interest as a shining black coach, drawn by two magnificently groomed and outfitted white horses, drew slowly up to a nearby curb. A most unusual, stately looking gentleman, sporting a black cane, climbed down from the driver's box, tethered the horses to a lamp post, and walked toward Joe. He moved briskly with a determined gait. What a spectacle! This guy looked like he had just stepped out of a Courier and Ives picture print. He was oddly dressed, but he was a pleasant-looking fellow with a gentle smile that seemed to glow from beneath a short, white moustache which blended at the corners of his mouth into the rest of the neatly trimmed, frosty whiskers that covered his jaws and chin. Joe was taken by the whiteness of that hair. No gray nor black showed; just pure white.

He was dressed to the nines, Joe thought. He didn't know exactly what that term meant, but it seemed to fit. He wore an old-fashioned, long-tailed green coat with enormous buttons. His dark trousers tapered into white spats that covered the tops and insteps of his black, spit-shined leather boots. Flung about his neck was a red plaid comforter which hung down to his waist, and the whole singular image was topped off with a tall, broad brimmed beaver hat. A sprig of green holly with red berries was tucked into the satin band.

It soon became clear that the bench Joe occupied was the old gentleman's destination. He stopped abruptly. His eyes twinkled above that quaint smile. His fingers barely touched the hat's brim in a sort of salute as he spoke.

"Good day my good man, and a merry Christmas to you!" he said, with a tone that was obviously affected by the spirit of the season. Then, without any invitation or hesitation, he sat down on the bench right next to Joe, who recoiled just a little from the man's brashness.

"Yea, sure," Joe stuttered, slightly shaken by the spectacle; then his natural assertiveness took over.

"Haven't I seen you somewhere before, like on a Christmas card or something?" Joe quipped.

"You very well may have," the old gentleman came back with a grin. "Oh, I love this wonderful season, don't you?" he enthused with a twinkle in his presence that seemed to dare Joe to disagree.

But Joe's well-disciplined forthrightness wouldn't lie.

"Not particularly," he grumbled honestly. "Who are you, anyway? And why are you all dressed up like that?" Joe believed in getting straight to the core of such things.

One of the old gent's eyes flashed a wink.

"Some of my friends call me Nick; and some say that I am the Spirit of Christmas personified. Actually though, I've retired from my previous occupation, and now all I do is drive that horse-drawn coach through this park, and thus share a little old-fashioned Christmas spirit with all these good people. That's the reason for this showy get-up.

"But I do, indeed, love Christmas!" the spectacle continued. "You might call me an ambassador for the season; or perhaps, in your lexicon, a public-relations man for the Prince of Peace, the gentle King whose birth gave rise to all this revelry which, apparently, you so disdain."

"I really don't disdain it," Joe mildly protested. "It's just that Christmas has never been something that I could really get into. Know what I mean?

"I guess it's the hypocrisy," Joe continued, sincerely trying to put into words the feelings with which he was, at that very moment, having such a struggle. "People just go crazy at this time of year, saying things they don't really mean, spending money they don't have for things they don't need, and for people they don't even like! It just seems to me that there should be more to it...or maybe there should be less to it!

"Besides," his voice trailed off, "no one has ever done any great Christmas favors for me."

"The answer lies in your focus, young man," the Coachman injected with knowing good humor. "You seem to concentrate on what other people do for you, or against you. But the precious secret of Christmas can be found only in what you do for others. You have obviously never heard the Christmas Bells ringing in your heart," he observed with confident boldness.

"Christmas Bells...in my heart? Not likely!" Joe chuckled cynically.

"No other feeling can equal it," said the Coachman, clamping a sincere grip on Joe's wrist. "No other sound can bring such joy, or such a wonderful feeling of worth! And this time of year, more than any other, offers so many fine opportunities to hear them!"

Well, this stuff was pure baloney as far as Joe was concerned. A large part of him was getting right near its edge of tolerance. In a more normal state he would just have written all of this off as merely the emotional superstition of the season and promptly removed himself from the presence of this wierd-looking character and his nutty sentiment; and most likely not too tactfully either. But, in some unexplainable way that seemed to be related to Joe's current condition, some small inner part of him seemed to sense some worth in the old guy's sincerity, if not in his actual philosophy. Bells ringing in the heart? Oh brother! Joe thought. But the old gentleman did have a way about him. And there was no doubt that, at least for a minute, he had Joe's attention.

"Say, you weren't kidding about being a good P.R. man," Joe grinned reluctantly. "Maybe there's something to what you're saying.

"Christmas Bells." Joe pondered the phrase. "Is that some kind of a figure of speech? Surely you don't mean that you believe someone could actually 'hear' bells ringing in his heart?" he asked skeptically.

"That's not an easy thing to describe, my boy." The Coachman's manner gently shifted from jovial to earnest. "It's more of a sensation; something you have to experience for yourself. But, if everything's in place, a person can, indeed, hear them ringing in his heart."

If Joe had thought more rationally about what he was doing he would have just left that park bench to this goofy intruder and never looked back. But there was a vibration down in the central core of where he lived which was causing a new sensation that was not all that unpleasant. Then the pleasantries ran head-on into rock-hard reality.

"Well, I could never feel anything like that," Joe confided with characteristic frankness. "I seem to be missing something that other people have. I've really noticed it lately, but I haven't been able to put my finger on it." His voice had turned from cynical to sad.

A look of puzzled interest crossed the features of Joe's face. He glanced around to be sure no one was watching, then he leaned closer to the Coachman.

"Man, this is crazy," he said in a lowered voice, "but do you think it would be possible. . .I mean after all these years of feeling only cold, competitive steel, do you think I could really hear bells in my heart and feel warmth in my gut?. . . you know, the feeling that I'm part of humanity; that I really have something worth giving; that I can actually share a part of myself with someone else?"

Joe was already having some new, unexpected experiences. He found himself pleading. Never before in his life had he done that. He had actually disclosed a tenderness that was dangerous in the world in which he lived, but it was refreshing, even invigorating! The old Coachman could have used it to hurt Joe, as others had done long before. Instead, he took a firmer hold of Joe's arm and looked directly into his eyes in a way that made the young man feel as though his very heart was being examined. Joe's spine danced with electricity as he listened with attention that was now focused with genuine interest.

"Joe," the Coachman said pointedly, "every living human being has not only the power, but also the right, to hear those bells! Infant or elder, wealthy or poor. Station in life is not a factor. The Savior's example and gift is for everyone. The state of an individual's heart holds the key."

Joe should have been startled at the sound of his own name coming from a total stranger. He couldn't remember introducing himself, but under the circumstances, it seemed perfectly natural.

"How did you know my name?" Joe asked, with an almost reverent interest.

"I have my ways," the Coachman smiled, with a touch of love and reassurance. "But that's not important. You and I have work to do."

It was beyond any limit of reason, but there was no doubt that Joe's interest was piqued. This old fellow knew what he was talking about, and Joe didn't doubt that it was from first-hand experience. It was incredible but, somehow, Joe trusted that this unlikely park-bench companion had the substance for which he had committed himself to search.

With the veneer of his pride tenderly peeled away, Joe was ready to be taught. He was oblivious to the time, to the cold of the winter afternoon, and to the totally unnatural circumstances. He temporarily put aside his lifetime collection of street-wise defenses, and like an innocent child fascinated by a bed-time story, Joe listened.

"You must follow the example of the Son of God and truly give of yourself," the Coachman patiently taught.

"Well, that would certainly be a new experience," Joe sighed. "How would I go about it? I don't even know where to begin." And he wasn't fooling.

"Quite simply put," said the Coachman, "just find someone who really needs you, and then give yourself unselfishly away. Now I realize that may seem overly simple, but it isn't as easy as it sounds. It may be the single most difficult thing you have ever done. But it's worth it!"

Again reality snapped Joe around.

"Well, that shoots it," he moaned. "There isn't anyone on this earth who needs me. They may need their jobs, or they may need my money; but no one really needs *me*."

"Everyone is needed by someone," the Coachman said without hesitation. "Have you looked around lately?"

"I wouldn't even know where to look," Joe said, "and even if I found the person, how would I know? I realize how terribly insensitive that must sound, but I'm telling you, I'm not too good at this sort of thing."

"If you're trying to be a tough nut, forget it Joe," the Coachman warned. "I'm not just a beginner, you know; and I'm not giving up on you. You're too valuable.

"Giving yourself away is hard enough, but sometimes it's almost as difficult to know when you're needed," the Coachman admitted. "I'm sure you've learned by now, though, that nothing worthwhile is easy. There are ways, but to find them, you must be willing to follow your heart. Let it listen and lead you. For the first time in your life, pay attention to your heart more than to your head; and when your heart hears the bells, it will whisper its wisdom to your mind, and you will know."

Joe stared into the brown grass of the winter park lawn, trying to let all this penetrate.

"Give it a try, my boy. It will change your life. It will provide for you that certain something for which you search, and it will enable all of the other good things you seek from life to happen. Once your heart has heard those bells, you will never again be the same.

"Well, what are you waiting for? There's no point in putting it off, and there's no better time to get started than right now with the tide of Christmas at its highest point and when the opportunities are so abundant." His clear old voice rang with conviction and his enthusiasm was catching.

The Coachman's tone quieted as he turned Joe and took him by both shoulders. The old, steel-blue eyes penetrated Joe's inner self as nothing ever had before.

"I give you my solemn promise, Joe," he firmly said, "that if you earnestly search for the means to truly give yourself away for the rest of this day, you will have the wonderful experience of hearing the Christmas Bells ring in your heart, and all of the other blessings the resulting change will bring, and all of this will happen before the sun rises on Christmas!"

3. Commitment

Emotion replaced reason with an incredible rush, and the need to hear those mysterious bells possessed Joe Turner. It wasn't that he actually believed that an old man dressed up in Christmas garb could change his life; and he wasn't exactly sure what it meant to give oneself away; but he couldn't deny the electricity he could still feel dancing along his spine every time he thought about the Coachman's promise. Feelings of anticipation had replaced the morose emptiness which he had felt just hours before and, as far as he was concerned, that was a giant step in the right direction. He was beginning to feel better already. He was at least as committed to the cause of hearing those bells as he had ever been to anything else he had ever done. That old guy really was some other kind of P.R. man, Joe chuckled inwardly. I could use him in the business, he thought, with amusement at the prospect.

Joe was totally serious, though, when he said that he didn't have the slightest idea about where to begin this strange adventure. He did reason, though, that whatever it was he was supposed to do was not likely to happen at a crowded, noisy Christmas Eve party. Especially one where everyone would surely go out of their way to avoid him and his reputation for being such a holiday sourpuss. He had to find a way out of that contrived obligation and get out on his own.

"Hello Susan," he said into the telephone to the faithful secretary who was still covering for him at the other end.

"Joe!" she blurted back into the phone as though it had suddenly become his face. "Are you OK? You've been gone for hours! We've been worried sick about you!"

"Take it easy, pal," Joe assured, "I'm OK. I just need a favor from you, and a whole bunch of understanding." He was using a voice that he intended to sound as though he was still moderately depressed.

"Well of course, silly, you know you can count on me. What do you need?" she responded with concern.

"You and Charlie are super for wanting to keep me in touch," Joe began, "but I'm going to have to stand you up for the office Christmas party tonight."

There was a perplexed pause while Susan forced that thought into focus.

"Oh no you don't, Joe Turner," she came back. "You're not going to weasel out of that party."

"No Susan, really I. . . ." Joe tried to interrupt, but she cut him off before he could get started.

"Come on, Joe," she countered. "We don't care if you don't play Santa Claus. That was a dirty trick and terrible timing, and we're sorry, but we've already decided that we're not going to let you spend Christmas Eve staying home with the cat. No way!"

What a woman, he thought. She's going to make a fine wife for somebody someday. . . but he'd wrestle with that thought later.

Susan was sharp, and if he wasn't careful she would see right through this ruse. He'd never even tried to be dishonest with her before, and this deception felt strangely uneasy; but this was so important to him right now. His course was set. He'd made his choice.

"No Sue, it isn't what you think. Do you remember my great aunt Harriet who lives upstate?" he asked. Before she could answer, he pressed on. "Well she called today, and she's lonely." His face winced at the lie, and he hoped it wouldn't telegraph through his voice.

"I've been kind of down lately, as you've probably guessed, and I'm feeling a real need for family." Oh, come on Joe, don't get corny on us or you'll really blow it, he warned himself. "I think it would be good for both her and me if I drove up to be with her tonight. You guys go ahead with the blast you've planned. Give everyone a nice gift and tell them I really do love and appreciate them. Just do your excellent thing, like you always do. I'll be back later tomorrow and we'll have dinner, OK?" She wasn't responding. He could tell she was processing all of the input, but he couldn't tell whether she was buying it or not. "You guys all have a good time, and tell all the vendors to send me the bill." Joe waited for a response.

"Sue, are you still with me?"

"Joe, are you sure you're all right?" She finally said. "Something sounds fishy." Man, she was sharp! She wasn't buying it. Joe knew he was a terrible liar. He'd learned long ago that the truth was always his best course.

"Yes, Sue dear, I'm all right. I appreciate your concern, I really do. I just have to go, OK?"

"Are you sure that's what you want to do?" She was still fishing for hidden meaning. This was some of the most unusual behavior she'd ever seen in this man she thought she knew so well.

"Well," she finally said in an obviously affected tone, "we wouldn't want to deprive aunt Harriet, of course." Then with a shift of feeling she added: "But we care about you too, you know."

Joe's heart skipped a little at the way that came through.

"I've got to do it, Sue," he said with finality. "You'll all probably be better off without me there anyway." Though he only meant that statement as bait for support, Joe was startled at how true the sound of it rang. They probably really would have more fun without him there to pull the cork on the spirit.

After the "see you laters," "drive carefullys" and all of those other pearls of wisdom and warning folks utter to loved ones before a departure, Joe hung up the receiver and congratulated himself. So Sue was skeptical. At least he was off the party hook. He was also growing increasingly aware that Susan meant more to him that he was willing to admit. He resolved then and there to never lie to her again, no matter how important the reason.

Now Joe turned, with all his energy, to the cause of those bells. Time was growing short, and he was serious.

But the main question he'd asked earlier hadn't gone away. What *did* he have to give?

Well he had money, he reasoned. Everyone needed that. He'd never given much of it away, but he was convinced that, if he could hear those bells ring in his heart and have his whole life changed, it would be worth a considerable price. It was certainly worth a try, as long as he didn't get too carried away with it, of course.

He literally ran back to his office to make the arrangements. This was the wildest thing he had ever planned, but he had made the commitment and he was going to do it. Nothing else had worked so far and, who knows, maybe it would actually be fun. It was already being a heady experience. Why hadn't he thought of it before?

Joe made sure no one saw him as he entered through the back door and made a quick visit to the safe where he kept some ready cash. He stuffed his wallet with fifteen brand new crisp one-hundred dollar bills and put it in his left breast pocket. He was as ready as he would ever be. He took a deep breath and ran to the street to hail a cab.

From his childhood he knew of a place in the city where there were plenty of people who didn't have much to look forward to at Christmas time. He resolved to start his self-giving experiment there.

As the cab jostled him along the busy city streets, Joe was aware of a variety of new sensations which flowed in and out and all around him. He even surprised himself when he tipped the cab driver generously and wished him a merry Christmas. So far, so good, he thought. This new me is really a pretty nice guy!

"Are you sure you don't want me to stick around for a while, Mac?" the cabby asked. "This isn't the safest part of town, ya know."

"No," Joe assured him. "I know these people. I grew up near here."

"OK, but don't say I didn't warn you." The dire tone of the cabby's voice made Joe smile, but a barely noticeable shiver of foreboding tingled along his spine just the same.

As the cab drove away Joe had yet another electrical surge of anticipation. He turned to the street to find his first mark.

"All right Mr. Coachman," he muttered out loud. "Bring on those Christmas Bells and let 'em ring!"

4. The Party

The mood at the office Christmas party was jovial but rather subdued. Everyone knew, of course, who was picking up the tab for this extravagant event, and they were grateful for his generosity, but they also knew full well who was really responsible for the bounteous refreshments and their lovely gifts from the company.

Susan and Charlie were perfect at hosting such an event. But tonight, close observers noticed their smiles seemed forced, or at least not as spontaneous as usual. Occasionally the two would exchange concerned glances, and Charlie would leave the room for a while. When he returned, they would meet for a moment and talk seriously.

"Well I let it ring thirty times, and he's still not answering," Charlie said in a low tone. "I think he's really gone somewhere to lay low."

"But where?" Susan responded with a troubled look. "I didn't buy that story about aunt Harriet for a minute, but I'm half tempted to call her just to tattle on him if nothing else."

"No, don't call," Charlie cautioned. "We both know he's not up there. It would just worry her needlessly.

"What concerns me most," he went on, "is what would he be doing with all that cash on him? He was being so cagey about getting it out of the safe. He was like a little kid stealing cookies."

"Whatever it is, I hope he gets through it all right." Susan's eyes misted as she spoke. "We've got to find something to help him with this Christmas thing he does. It's getting worse every year. If something doesn't change the downward spiral he could soon be featured as the main character in a Charles Dickens Christmas ghost story."

"Well, we tried," Charlie pointed out. "And although I feel for the nerd, and I totally agree with you, he's a big boy, and if he doesn't want us butting in he's just going to have to work it out by himself." Susan would have taken issue with the seeming finality of that statement, but she knew Charlie didn't really mean it. Besides, they couldn't let Joe's eccentricity ruin the evening for the faithful employees who had worked hard all year, and who deserved this recognition so much.

In spite of her attempts to be totally professional in matters involving her boss, tears fogged Susan's eyes every time she thought about him and whatever it was he was going through tonight.

Just as the party seemed to be winding down prematurely, the lid nearly blew off the place when the door flew open and there stood a little five-foot-one-inch, ninety-eight-pound Santa Claus in the infamous red suit from the office coat closet. It couldn't have been more perfectly timed. For a minute, no one knew who it was, and then there was a recognition.

"Mildred!" someone yelled from the back of the room, and the whole scene fell apart in raucous laughter. She'd let the bun down from the back of her head and curly grayish-white hair fell convincingly from the large red cap to her shoulders. Unfortunately, even with pillows and wadded up newspaper padding, the huge suit still hung in comical drapes over her tiny frame.

No one could believe it! The place went wild as she danced into the room Ho-Ho-Ho-ing in a silly deep voice and fishing wrapped, home-made candy from a gunny-sack to distribute to her laughing, cheering colleagues. Tears rolled down their cheeks and their sides ached until they couldn't draw a breath.

Well that started things rolling with an earnest festivity that caused even Sue and Charlie to put their concerns aside. Now, the re-charged, unforgettable gala would continue, un-interrupted, well into the early hours of Christmas!

5. Another View of Christmas

As in most cities of any size, this one had run-down, dilapidated corners with residents for whom Christmas was only a grim reminder of life's hopelessness. Given the opportunity, most of them would have gladly traded, problem for problem, for Joe Turner's Christmas turmoil. The lives and lifestyles of these inner-city inhabitants were so far removed from Joe's that they may as well have been on another planet.

Their lives required a lot of leaning. They leaned against walls, against lamp posts, against society, and against each other. When they did walk, it was with more of a causeless shuffle than a need to get anywhere. There were individual exceptions, of course. But for most of them, being merry was only a figure of speech that was used with mockery and sarcasm. Perhaps that was why the four sinister-looking men who abruptly entered the scene stood out with such contrast. If nothing else, they had purpose.

With cat-like movements the one who wore a moustache and trench coat, which were both as dark as his mood, stepped out of the darkness into a circle of light under a dim street lamp. He pressed close to two other male figures who flinched involuntarily in reaction to his familiar but un-welcomed intrusion. The main victim of his intrusion was a younger man with clean-cut, square-jawed features and dark, curly hair. The other was the young man's little eight-year-old brother.

The leader of the sinister squad gripped the young man's arm and jerked it violently into a hammer lock.

"Merry Christmas, Anthony!" a gruff, accented voice growled menacingly into the young man's ear. "How about if you give your old friend Max a five-hundred dollar Christmas present."

"All my friends call me Tony," the younger man grimaced with a practiced resolve. He'd felt the pain of the strong hold before and knew very well what it meant.

"Well now, what does that tell you, ANTHONY?" the menacing voice emphasized. "It could mean that people who owe me money ain't my friends, and Anthony my boy, you know what I do to my enemies ain't pretty."

When the young man writhed against the pain in his shoulder the three sinister colleagues tightened their circle around him. His younger brother backed into an arched doorway to watch in frightened silence.

"You were friendly enough when you loaned me the money," the young man said through clenched teeth. Then, with a single violent tug, he wrenched free from the painful hold and drew backward to confront his challengers.

"That was last month, punk," the aggressor spat. "But now it's pay-up time. We had an agreement, remember? It's the holiday season when you're supposed to give generously," he taunted. "I'm usually a patient, loving man, Anthony, but interest has just jumped your original loan from five-hundred bucks up six-hundred, and my patience is wearing thin."

"Look, my grandmother is really sick, Max," the young man plead. "You know I needed the money for medicine. I didn't just blow it; and you know I'm out of work. Where am I going to get six-hundred dollars right now?"

"You shoulda' thought of that last month, Tony boy," the hood sneered coldly. "Sounds to me like you got yourself a little problem."

"Come on Max, you know I'm good for it," the young man protested. "I said I'd pay back every cent, and I will. Just give me a little more time."

"Look punk," the rough voice continued, "I'm tired of foolin' around. But since it's Christmas, and since I'm such a Christian fellow, I'll give you until midnight tomorrow, and if I don't have that dough by then, your grandmother will definitely need medicine."

Blood rushed to Tony's head. The powerful muscles in his arms hardened as his fists clenched in anger and frustration.

"What does that mean?" he asked, already knowing the awful answer.

"Get smart, kid," the hoodlum smirked. "That means that, if we have to, we lean on the sweet old lady a little to convince you to pay up."

"You keep your hands off my grandmother, Max. She didn't do anything," the young man tried to reason. "I'm not letting you anywhere near her."

"You can't watch her every second, punk," the shady character replied. "It would be a shame to have to give your little brother Stevie there a broke-up grandma for Christmas, now wouldn't it," he said, nodding toward the boy, who instinctively moved further back into the shadow of the doorway.

"Now just get the money and save all of us a lot of trouble. Do you understand, ANTHONY?"

"I hear you, Max," the younger man said in submission. "I'll get it to you by midnight tomorrow." The futility of furthering the argument was clear. From a lifetime of experience, Tony understood the rules. In a foolish, but well-intended panic he'd borrowed the money, and now it was time to pay it back. If he didn't there would, indeed, be trouble. That's how it worked on the street.

"Max is a creep," the younger boy muttered angrily as the sinister brotherhood disappeared into the darkness. "We can't let him hurt Ma." His voice quivered as they walked.

"Take it easy, Stevie," the big brother tried to comfort. "He isn't going to hurt Ma. You know I had to borrow the money for the medicine. There was no other way. But I'm going to pay it back tomorrow."

"Where are you going to get six hundred dollars, Tony," the boy asked warily, "when we don't even have enough money to buy Ma a Christmas present?"

"You leave that to me, pal," Tony assured. His face and voice showed admirable determination, but the net effect was slightly diffused with a tinge of uneasiness. "We'll pay back the money and get Ma a present too. Trust me. Have I ever let you down before?

"Just don't tell her about this," Tony cautioned. "It would only worry her, and she doesn't need that right now, OK?"

"OK," the boy said trustingly. "But just promise me you won't do anything stupid."

"I won't, kid," the big brother promised with a good natured smile and a tousle of the boy's hair. But a troubled look crossed his well-formed jaw, even as he spoke it.

Ever since the terrible accident that had taken both their parents, Tony had worked hard and done his best to help their grandmother who had taken them into her poor, but loving, inner-city home. Things were good while he had work and she had her health. Going part-time, he had even been able to get in a year of business school, with good grades too; but then this strange illness robbed her of her vitality, and he lost his job.

He had the personal satisfaction of knowing that he'd worked hard and done his best, and he knew that he'd shown great promise in the business world. But how could he have known that his bookkeeper boss would grab all the company's money and skip town? The business folded, of course, and now, on Christmas eve, Tony Merino was not only out of work and in debt and trouble up to his ears, but his reputation had been shattered beyond repair. Time after time he went for job interviews, and everyone was initially interested in him; but as soon as they learned who he'd worked for, as they inevitably did, he was immediately turned away. Even though they said they didn't blame him personally, no one wanted to take a chance.

Forced by desperation, his troubled mind formed an otherwise unthinkable plan. It shook his conscience and every value he possessed, but he'd tried everything else without success; there was no way those thugs were going to get their hands on his grandmother.

"Stevie," he said, "I need you to go home and stay with Ma until I get back."

"No Tony, I want to come with you," the little brother whined, almost as if he knew by a premonition that something bad was about to happen.

"Come on now, do as I say, kid. I won't be that long. It's Christmas Eve and Ma needs us home, but first there's something I gotta do. I'll see you in an hour or so."

"Will you bring Ma a present?" the boy asked.

"Yea, I'll bring Ma a present, and maybe even one for you," Tony smiled nervously. "But right now you have to do as I say."

He left the boy at the entrance of the narrow old brownstone where they lived and quickly slipped back out onto the darkened street.

Half way down the next block he realized, without much surprise, that he was being followed. He ducked into a doorway and waited. It was only seconds before Stevie crept past, craftily trying to keep out of sight. The boy yelped in startled surprise as Tony's arm shot out from the darkness and reeled him in.

"Stevie, what are you trying to do?" the older brother shot the words out as he held the boy by both shoulders at arms length. "I said stay with Ma! Now get back there and do as you're told before I kick the stuffin' out of you!"

"But Tony. . . ." the boy tried to protest.

"But Tony nothin'. You get home!"

"OK, I'll go," the boy lied in fake submission. "But please just don't do anything crazy!" The boy resolved inwardly that he'd be more careful. He wasn't about to let his big brother out of his sight in his present mental state.

"Christmas makes people crazy," Tony mumbled, more to himself than to his little brother. "But sometimes you've just gotta do what you've gotta do," he said with a quick hug. He was suddenly overcome with the realization of how much he loved that little kid and of how vulnerable he and his aging grandmother were. Tony knew it was all up to him now. He choked on the emotion that erupted to the surface and blinked back rare tears as he abruptly turned and hurried away without looking back. He knew if he did he would surely lose his nerve to go through with his awful, but seemingly necessary plan for survival.

6. The Gifts

As he came to the first street corner, Joe paused momentarily to consider his next move. He flinched involuntarily as he felt a hand on his shoulder from behind. He spun around and was about to cock his arm to throw a punch when he saw the whiskered face of one of the most dejected men he had ever seen. A battered old hat fell limply over one eye, and a bony knee protruded through a hole in his ragged trouser.

The man was near tears as, in a quivering voice, he told the story of his destitute condition; his poor, sick wife and starving children, and, of course, him with no work. The story ended, as Joe knew it would, with the trembling voice pleading for cash.

Well, this must be it. Joe listened, almost believing that he would actually hear bells. All he heard was the siren of a police patrol car several blocks away. He wrestled with the realization that he was actually doing this.

Well there was no doubt that this guy needed help, so why not start here?

You should have seen those two bleary eyes pop at the sight of that brand new one hundred-dollar bill with not so much as a wrinkle in it. The ragged figure almost tripped over himself as he skipped down the street, leaving Joe to wonder about the experience. There were certainly no bells, and it wasn't satisfying at all watching one hundred of his hard-earned dollars dance away in that unkempt fist. Not only that, the red-nosed old bum didn't even say thanks!

Interested now in seeing how such a man would handle his new-found wealth, Joe followed at a reasonable distance. The shabby figure's destination was an equally shabby bar.

"What a zinger," Joe uttered. As he passed the open door he heard a shout ring through the smokey din.

"Oh wow, mates! I plucked a fat chicken! I'm rich! The drinks are on me!"

Joe shook his head in disgust and moved on. Surely *that* wasn't what the Coachman had in mind.

Joe wasn't a quitter, but he walked several more blocks before he decided to try the expensive experiment again.

His next potential recipient was sitting on the sidewalk with his back against the graffiti-smeared wall of a grimy building. This time he was a much younger man, but just as poorly situated as the first.

"Whatever happened to motivation and self-respect," Joe mumbled in despair. He just couldn't understand why a man would allow that condition to come into his life.

"Could you spare the price of a Christmas meal?" the candidate asked as Joe approached. "I haven't eaten decent in a week."

From the look of him, Joe could believe it. Again he listened; this time with a degree of hope as well as forced belief. The only sound that distinguished itself from the rest of the street noises was an agitated dog barking somewhere in the distance. Joe shrugged, but he'd made the commitment and he didn't intend to quit yet.

Once again there were widened eyes, but this time there was also a profuse series of "thank-you-sirs" and bowing and carrying on to the point of embarrassment. Joe was afraid the man was going to give him a big kiss right on the mouth. He got ready to duck. Instead, the character ran off down the street with his un-wrinkled, green-backed treasure.

Again Joe followed. This fellow ran directly to an alley, at the end of which a motley group was all huddled over something. As Joe approached, he saw his recent beneficiary already walking slowly away with his head hung low. The man spotted Joe and hesitated, then he did an absolutely unbelievable thing. He came right up to his apparent wellspring of wealth and boldly asked if he would happen to have another of those "lovely leaves of lettuce" he could borrow. . ."just until tomorrow." In response to Joe's inquiry as to the whereabouts of the first one, the man explained how he'd figured that with his luck running so good, he could easily parlay his single blessing into twins at this roving crap game; but, alas, fate was not on his side!

Joe shot back a heart-felt "Get lost, creep!" and moved on.

This project was not getting any easier. In fact, it was downright depressing. Daylight was gone, and it seemed to have taken with it all of the warmth of life. Joe pulled the collar of his overcoat up around his ears against the bitter breeze. He decided that next time he would be more selective. The Coachman was right. Giving yourself away isn't as easy as it sounds.

The next opportunity came abruptly as the door to a large old building opened and a portly middle-aged woman exited to the sidewalk. She was grumbling something about selfish prudes and lack of consideration keeping a body working so late on the Eve of Christmas; and all that just so's they could junk it up again tomorrow with a party for their spoiled-brat offspring. Without looking, she turned suddenly into Joe's path and nearly ran over him. In spite of everything, Joe tried to be cheery.

"Good evening dear lady, and a merry Christmas!"

"Well I s'pose for some it is," grumped the woman. "Seems like them that has, gets; and the rest of us has to go on feelin' like the bottom of the garbage heap. To them, we're no more'n common slaves."

Well she obviously wasn't rolling in Rolls Royces either, but she seemed to be industrious, and was certainly in better shape than the last two candidates. Joe walked along beside her to see what he could learn.

"What are you up to, young man, out so late on Christmas Eve? Don't you have no kin?"

"Well my dear, I was looking for you," Joe said.

"For me? What on earth for?" she questioned.

Was now the time? Joe listened. Through an upper story window across the street came the sound of an angry mother yelling full voice at a wayward child. That was all he heard.

Oh well, why not? This one at least seemed deserving, and even in her grumpiness, Joe was sure she would put his money to good use.

"I have a gift for you to brighten your holiday." Joe tried to be pleasant as he tucked the new bill into the shopping bag she carried.

The woman stopped abruptly and fished the treasure out. As she examined it carefully, her furrowing brow narrowed her eyes to a squint.

"Is it funny money?" she asked, turning it over and over suspiciously with her head half ducked.

"No, it's real!" Joe declared with a sort of hurt tone in his voice.

"Is it honest earned, or is it dirty?" the woman persisted.

"I earned it!" Joe protested, getting a little impatient. "I earned it honestly, its real, and I want you to have it."

"Why me? What have I done for you? What are you up to, young man? What do you want from me? Are you makin' improper advances?" Her mood was getting agitated.

"I resent that insinuation, lady," Joe said defensively. "I have plenty of money and I just thought you'd. . . ."

"You just thought, did you!" the woman interrupted. "Well now you listen, sonny! I work hard for my keep, and I do all right by myself! I don't need any fancy dressed do-gooder comin' down here and tryin' to work any charities on me! You can take your filthy means, that are probably ill-begotten anyway, and go salve your conscience on somebody else!"

With that exclamation she crumpled up that brand new one hundred-dollar bill and threw it right into Joe's astonished face!

"Well, I'll be!" Joe blurted. "You're crazy, woman! The whole ungrateful lot of you are crazy!"

Joe's commitment waned. He'd had enough. To vent the exasperation that had been building for too long now, he turned to the street, which by now was nearly deserted except for the broad backside of the cleaning woman disappearing through a doorway, and yelled "YOU CAN ALL TAKE CHRISTMAS AND STOMP ON IT!"

7. The Checkered Coat

"Christmas Bells! Baloney!" All Joe had heard so far was a siren, a dog barking, and a woman yelling at her kid. This seedy neighborhood was giving him the creeps. The whole earth had gone bonkers. What was he doing here trying to work a crummy experiment anyway? People weren't worth it. Even wearing the dumb red suit would have been better than this. He was cold, he was lonely and, wouldn't you know it, now there wasn't even a cab in sight.

He turned on Gulf Street to head toward home. It was dimly lit and deserted. By now Joe's thoughts had turned downright caustic.

"The whole human race is nothing but a herd of turkeys!" he grumbled to himself. "I'd have been better off throwing my money down a rat hole. At least a rat wouldn't...."

Joe's thoughts were cut short violently! A cold, bare hand that felt like a meat hook suddenly clamped itself over his mouth and nose. He could barely see that it was attached to an arm in an old, checkered green coat. It was a muscular arm that felt like it was made of iron. It had come from out of nowhere. He couldn't turn his head to see who was on the other end of it, but whoever it was was dragging him backward into the shadows of an alley!

As he struggled for air, his pounding heart nearly stopped as he felt something hard jab a sharp pain into his ribs from behind, and a gruff, disguised voice whispered, "That's a gun you feel in your back, man. Take it easy and you won't get hurt. All I want is your wallet and your watch."

The feeling seeped out of Joe's neck and shoulders as his air supply dwindled. His strength dissolved into numbness, and he couldn't think or move. This guy really meant business!

Reality spun into blackness. The sound of running footsteps faded into the distance, and then everything was quiet.

Joe gradually became aware that he was still breathing, because when he did it, it hurt like the dickens. He was lying, face down, in a pile of something soft and foul smelling. A nearly empty booze bottle was dumping the remainder of its repulsive contents down his neck.

"Garbage!" The word forced itself out of his pain-racked throat. He was almost sobbing.

Joe's whole body throbbed with a pain that pulsated through him but didn't seem to be centered anywhere in particular. He slowly stood up, and his feet slipped on something slimy before they found solid pavement. His senses finally began to piece together what had happened. Street-wise Joe Turner had been mugged. His trembling hand felt for his inside vest pocket. Empty! His wallet, and the small fortune it contained, was gone.

"Oh great!" he cussed out loud. "What a perfect ending for a totally rotten experience. I should have known. So much for the old Christmas Clown's theory. The world has proven him wrong. Reality wins again!"

Once again he yelled at the street, and this time with a vengeance.

"CHRISTMAS IS THE PITS, AND ALL OF MANKIND IS WORSE!"

It was just about then he realized he didn't even have a quarter for a phone call.

It seemed to be awfully late. He checked his watch. It wasn't there either. His wrist, where it had been, was stinging terribly with what felt like fingernail gouges.

"Well, at least I'm alive," he mumbled, trying desperately to find something to be grateful for.

As he stumbled back toward the open street, the form of a small person, probably a child, darted from the shadows and around the corner of the building. Surely that couldn't have been the criminal.

"Wait! Stop!" Joe yelled. "I've been mugged!" No use. The form was gone.

Joe stumbled into the light of a dim street lamp. His clothes were disheveled and stained. His face contorted at the odor. He smelled like a cheap brewery.

About two blocks down he saw two men enter the doorway of what looked like a bar. He heard laughter and the music from a jukebox. As repulsive as going in there was to him, that place was probably his only salvation. He pushed his way into the small, dimly lit room that was crowded with Christmas Eve revelers. How disgusting, he thought.

He worked his way up to the bartender to explain his predicament and to see if he could get some help. The man he stood next to reached into a patch of light on the counter for some change. Joe's heart skipped at what he saw. It was the coat! The same checkered green coat which was on the arm that had grabbed him!

Now Joe's intense competitive instincts, sharpened by his recent experience, took over. Without even thinking of the possible consequences, he spun the owner of the coat and arm around. It was a big man with a jovial, though slightly sodden, face. He wore a cap which bore the logo of a trucking company.

"Give me my money back!" Joe demanded, in a yell that quieted the whole place.

"What are you talking about?" the startled face asked.

"Don't give me that, you creep! You know what I'm talking about! You ripped me off, and I want my money back!"

Joe's temper really cut loose. Now, along with his enraged screaming, he was swinging. . . .

Well, in all fairness to Joe, it was dark in that alley, and how could he have known that he was accusing the wrong man? In any event, the coat only *looked* like the one his attacker wore; and the big truck driver he was assaulting was very strong. The fight that ensued was violent, but brief. The next thing Joe knew, he was being shackled and hauled away in the caged back seat of a black and white police cruiser.

He ducked his head to avoid the gaze of the irate spectators who shook their fists and shouted obscenities at him. How humiliating. Could anything be worse?

8. The Christmas Eve Jail

The precinct jail was a popular place on this eve of the big holiday. Joe tried, of course, to explain who he was and what he was doing there, but the desk officer was not very patient. He was particularly amused when Joe gave his name.

"It never ceases to amaze me how fast news travels through the inner circle," the officer said. "You retrieve a wallet which has been ripped off an honest man, and every bum on the street comes in to claim it."

"You mean you have my wallet?" Joe demanded. "Where did you get it?"

"You're fourth in line, Bud," the hassled officer said.

"But it has my name in it!" Joe protested.

"Yea, I know; Joe Turner, right?" So far there are four of you. The first one who can prove it, gets it. In the meantime, you're charged with public intoxication, disorderly conduct, disturbing the peace, and assault on a private citizen; so you might as well go back with the rest of the bums and sleep it off. Smells like you could use it!"

"You!... You!..." Joe stammered in futility.

"Hold it Mac," the weary officer cautioned. "Anything you say or do is just gonna make it worse."

In utter disbelief, Joe saw the hopelessness of the situation. More fighting would, indeed, only make it worse; and worse was what he didn't need it to be right now.

"Can't I at least make a phone call?" he asked, in as calm a voice as he could manage.

"Yea, you can make one call, but that's all until morning...next!"

Charlie's phone rang twelve times before Joe remembered the office Christmas party—the one he'd so skillfully ditched. He slowly lowered the receiver of the battered wall phone to its cradle, almost overcome with desperation. Oh, if he'd just agreed to wear that dumb red suit, none of this would have happened.

He looked at the big, cold, official-looking clock on the wall. 12:30 a.m. Charlie wouldn't be home for two or three more hours, nor would Susan, or anyone else he knew. He may not even be able to reach them in the morning, being Christmas and all, and no one would think to look for him. He wished desperately, now, that Susan had nailed him in that lie. Thanks to his genius, they all thought he was upstate with great-aunt Harriet.

"Fantastic!" Joe slammed his fist down hard on the counter. A sharp pain of reality shot up his arm.

"OK, take me away," he mumbled. "It fits perfectly with everything else that's happened tonight."

Hard working, well-meaning, law abiding, mostly honest, Joe Turner was led to a cell to spend his would-be life-changing Christmas Eve in jail.

The woebegone inmate population was twice as large as the jail's capacity, as it was on nearly every holiday. A morose jailer with a large ring of keys dangling from his belt locked Joe in a cell in the middle of a bar-lined hallway. Joe soon discovered he had three roommates. Two were drunks who were so far gone they didn't even know he was there, but the other one was a sullen, good-looking young man with a square jaw and black, curly hair. Joe figured him to be probably twenty-one or twenty-two years old. He was sturdily built and almost clean-cut. Neither of them spoke. Each had plenty to think about.

Joe paced. The younger man just laid on the soiled mattress of a top bunk in the semi-darkness and stared at an invisible spot on the ceiling.

The hopeless confinement pressed into Joe's nerves in ways that he wouldn't have guessed. After what seemed like an hour or so, he couldn't stand the silence any longer.

"What are you in for, kid?" he asked abruptly.

After a long pause, a terse answer came reluctantly.

"I made a big mistake."

"Come here often?" Joe tried to quip.

"Nope. First time. But this is a big one. I've done some dumb things, but never anything like this."

"You have people?" Joe asked.

There was another significant stretch of silence, and then the young man spoke slowly, almost painfully, with lengthy pauses between each short comment.

"A little brother and a grandmother who's raised us.... She's very sick...I'm not sure she's gonna make it...." Those last words choked with emotion.

Then there was more silence.

"Got a job?" Joe finally pressed, more to keep the terrible silence away than to satisfy any curiosity.

"Nope. Had one, but the company folded. I've tried hard, but things are tough."

Joe wrestled for understanding. The young man seemed bright and capable. In fact, he was the kind of a kid who, if the circumstances were different, would make a great employee—even a great partner. What a waste. What is this crazy world doing to us, he thought.

Through the long night the door to the outer area opened with regularity and the two harried jailers were kept busy ushering new guests into the already crowded quarters.

At 3:30 a.m. Joe asked if he could place his call again. He could hear grumbling out in the foyer, but he was finally permitted to leave the cell and go to the battered phone. There was still no answer.

Back in the cell again, there was still no voluntary comment from the brooding kid.

"Charlie's always been a party bum," Joe mumbled almost to himself.

Except for the snoring of the two drunks, there was only more of the dismal, dreaded silence.

Joe stood holding the bars, his face toward the hallway. He had to force-feed his mind with pleasant thoughts to keep from going crazy. A slight smile crossed his face as he thought of Mildred, the woman with the bun on her head, who had drawn the impossible job of asking him to play Santa Claus. He shouldn't have been so rough on her, but that look on her face when he'd pretended to stumble onto their secret was amusing. Why, he'd heard them whispering about that for days.

Mildred was an efficient, straight-arrow woman if there ever was one. She'd never married anyone except her job. Maybe that was why she was such an excellent employee. He should compliment her occasionally and warm her up a little, but he had a feeling that ice water ran in her veins. Even though she was one of the first employees he had hired, and she had faithfully supported him all this time, he didn't really know her. She was just one more person with whom he had never been able to establish a relationship. But who could relate with a prune, he reasoned.

Susan loved Mildred; but then Susan loved everybody. Liquid sunshine ran in Susan's veins. She was warm, radiant, beautiful. . . . Joe pictured her in his mind. Now there was a pleasant thought—her auburn hair bouncing that certain way when she walked, her soft green eyes, her peaches-and-cream skin, and the marvelous way it was all put together! Never had he known such a woman. But he couldn't really tell her how he felt about her either. If there was only some way he could straighten himself out inside so he would be worthy of someone like that. . . .

Reality forced its way back into his mind. The dark-haired kid was really depressed, and Joe wasn't in great emotional shape either. His thoughts wandered back to the dark side. What is the reason for this mockery? Where is justice? Two promising young men stuck in a jail cell with two totally useless sots for Christmas Eve! And what about the merciless jerk who ripped him off? With the way the legal system worked, they would probably just rap his worthless knuckles and turn him back to the street to hit again. Next time he'd probably kill somebody.

Oh, that animal. Imagine, a cowardly attack in the dark, and from the back! How Joe yearned to be able to meet him face to face, just for two minutes. That's all it would take!...

Once again the door to the outer area opened, and through it Joe could see the big, cold clock. It was 4:30 a.m. Finally, after passing pleas to the desk officer through the jailer with the big key ring, Joe was allowed to try his call once more.

This time, thank heaven (if there was such a place), after Joe had lost count of the number of rings, a sleepy voice mumbled something incoherently at the other end.

"Charlie!" Joe erupted. "Where the samhill have you been? Man, you're not gonna believe this, but I need you bad!..."

It was with considerable relief that Joe returned to the cell this time. He couldn't stifle a persistent little grin that kept creeping out of its box onto his face. Finally things were starting to move in the right direction.

The kid was still awake and lying in that unchanged position, staring at that same invisible spot.

"Well, I finally got to my man. He'll be coming for me soon. Any one I can call for you when I get out?" Joe asked. Somehow he felt obligated to ask.

By now, he was used to the long pauses. This kid didn't just jump into anything.

"Thanks, but it's no use," the kid finally responded. "I won't be needing anything for a long time."

"Why?" Joe finally let out the question that he'd been restraining all night. "What did you do to get yourself so down? Surely it can't be that bad."

Joe wanted to congratulate himself for feeling something for this poor kid, but he had to admit that his interest was mainly curiosity.

It was clear the kid really didn't want to talk about it, and there was another protracted period of silence. But then, suddenly, it was as though someone pulled the chain on a plug. The barrier fell away, and the words spilled out in a torrent.

"OK, I blew it! Some guys were pressing me for a bill I owe for my grandma's medicine. They were going to use her for a punching bag. I lost my cool. Last night I grabbed a guy over on Gulf Street. I stuck a stick in his ribs and told him it was a gun." The kid struggled as his voice choked with emotion. "I ripped off his watch and wallet. It turned out he was loaded. The cops caught my little brother and made him talk. They picked me up not ten minutes later."

The reality of those words slammed into Joe's sensibilities with megaton force! He felt like he'd been hit in the stomach with a baseball bat. Reflex was about to turn him around swinging but, fortunately, a smattering of reason leaped out of the darkness and restrained him. His jaw muscles twitched with the rhythmic clenching of his teeth as the young man continued to reveal his woe.

"Oh, man," the kid moaned, now nearly in tears. "I've done some crazy things, but never anything like this. When that guy shows up outside to claim his things, he'll press charges for armed robbery, and I've had it! I'm guilty and they know it. I don't have a chance."

There it was! The whole sordid thing laid out right there before him in a jail cell. The culmination! The climax of the last twelve hours of humiliation and pain.

His mind screamed in silence, THIS KID, RIGHT HERE WITHIN ARM'S REACH, IS THE VERY CREEP WHO RIPPED ME OFF!

It felt like all of Joe's blood surged to his head. This punk, this vicious young animal, was the very one he'd yearned to get his hands on! The pains in Joe's neck and arms, his bruised ribs, his stolen money, his battered ego; all begged for revenge.   A sick grandmother! Oh sure! How many times had he heard that line, with slight variations, in the last twelve hours? These guys all have it memorized. The kid's a monster, just like all the rest.

Recollections of the hook-like hand and the checkered coat flashed through Joe's mind. His instincts fought to break free— to hit and kick and hammer until all of the hurt he felt was transferred to this. . .this CREEP!

Joe's mind swirled in a frenzy of thought. Fortunately, reason, again, forced its way through his tortured self. Stay cool, Joe. Keep your mouth shut. You're in jail, remember. There's a better way. Charlie's good. He can really sew this guy up. Anything you do out of blind rage will just mess things up.

Except for his steel-gray stare, and the twitch in his jaw muscles, Joe kept the raging conflict within, but it was right on the edge. The creepy kid had better not push it!

Joe wrestled to keep his temper in a hammer lock. Charlie will be here soon. He'll make the identification and get the release, and then they can put the clamps on this worthless hunk of meat for good. That will be almost as satisfying as punching out his stupid headlights. We don't need more violence, Joe reminded himself. There had been enough of that already.

The Bells of Christmas! What a farce. What a dream of fools. The world is a zoo! Now Joe remembered why he'd never resorted to mushy sentimentality.

Joe's knuckles were white from clenching the bars. The hard, cold metal pressed into his forehead. What in blazes was keeping that screw-ball lawyer? Temptations of temper swept over him in waves. He had to get out of this place! He had to get away from this miserable monster who had caused him so much agony; away from the barren hopelessness of this jail; and away from the sickening odors, from his thoughts, and particularly from those persistent, haunting words of the old Coachman that would just not leave him alone.

". . .the Bells of Christmas. Listen, and you will know."

Listen, bull! He listened all right and, thanks to the old goat in the comical Christmas suit, all he heard now were the forlorn early morning sounds of an overworked city jail: the sob of a forgotten derelict, the retching of a drunk, the flushing of an open toilet, the clank of stainless steel utensils on a metal tray.

"Oh Charlie, where are you?" he whispered through clenched teeth.

Finally, after an eternity of torment, the door to the outer area opened, and a tired-looking jailer came and unlocked the heavy, barred door.

"You've been sprung, Mac," he said. "You can go."

Sweeter-sounding words had never touched Joe's ears. He exited quickly, without a word to his silent companion who was still prostrate on the cot. The door shut again with a solid clank, and Joe was free; free to perform a very satisfying citizen's duty. He could already taste the succulence of revenge. It had never been sweeter!

The door to the outer area opened and he could hardly believe what he saw. There stood Charlie, looking like someone had yanked him out of bed in the middle of a nightmare. He wore one brown shoe and one black one. His fly was un-zipped, and half of the tail of his striped pajama top draped, un-tucked, from his pants. Even if he did have to stifle a laugh, Joe had never seen him look so good.

"Charlie, you gotta help me throw the book at a guy!" Joe began before Charlie could spout off about the party deception or smart-mouth about anything else. "He's back there in the cell. The scum mugged me and ripped me off! You see, there was this old Coachman in the park, and...."

9. The Bells

A relieved, and very satisfied, Joe Turner was just putting his signature on the paperwork that would seal doom upon the fate of the creep in the jail cell who he thought to be one of the lowest forms of life. We've all got to work together, he thought, to keep that kind of refuse where it belongs. We've got to make that kid an example so all of the other punks will get the message. . . .

His ears were busy with revenge and officialdom and a flood of questions from Charlie. But, from somewhere, his heart picked up a faint sound and singled it out from the rest. Though muffled and barely audible in the official din, it was unmistakably the notes of chiming bells.

Joe lifted his pen for a second and listened.

"What is that sound? Do I hear bells?" he asked incredulously.

"I don't hear anything," Charlie replied. He looked at the desk officer, who shrugged negatively. "Probably the result of a tough night," Charlie theorized.

"No wait," Joe persisted. "I know I heard bells. . .listen."

As everyone listened, the sound of beautiful, chiming bells filled the room from somewhere outside.

It was the desk officer who finally replied.

"Oh, those bells," he smiled. "I hadn't noticed until you mentioned it. Those are the bells from the old St. Christopher's Church across the street, Mr. Turner. They always begin to play just before the sun rises, to ring in Christmas. We call them the Christmas Bells."

A sudden impact jolted Joe as a distinct memory replayed itself on the tape deck of his mind. It was the words of the Coachman.

"I give you my solemn promise," it whispered, ". . . before the sun rises on Christmas. . . ."

"The CHRISTMAS BELLS! Oh come on!" Joe stammered. He glanced around into the faces of the people who surrounded him, in disbelief. There was no denying it, his heart had heard those bells clearly and distinctly before anyone else could hear them; and, in spite of his greatest efforts to block it out, a gradual, but crescendoing illumination came, just as the old Coachman had said it would.

Joe's combative instincts reacted violently and fought back. No! Not now! they screamed. Not the creep! This can't be the time! It's just a crazy coincidence!

But in spite of everything intelligent and rational, Joe couldn't resist. He finally knew, with certainty, how he could truly give himself away. His promised opportunity for a Christ-like act of pure, selfless giving was back there locked in the same jail cell in which he had spent the horrible night! It was so plain! How could he have been so blind? He would unconditionally forgive and let him go!

Joe was visibly shaken as the consequences of that monumental decision jerked him through the whole spectrum of emotion. The dam of a lifetime of emotional self-defense ruptured, and a cascade of truth burst forth. Persistent, pure knowledge, that could not be turned back, coursed through sub-conscious channels throughout Joe's fiber. His emptiness soaked it up like a thirsty sponge.

Joe slowly stood erect. His gaze was fixed somewhere in inner space. The gate that had kept sensitivity out of his system for so long had been blown from its hinges. He trembled visibly as slender, gentle fingers of love reached deep into his soul and peeled back layer after layer of calloused, egocentric self; and light poured into places it had never been before.

In a miraculous instant he knew it all with absolute surety. He knew what he was now able to give to a loving relationship with Susan; he knew where he could confidently turn for the help he so desperately needed in his work; and he knew how he could, indeed, claim his coveted membership in the human race! He knew it all, and, not only that, now he could do it! With that one incredible decision to overcome pride, ego, revenge, and a dozen other lusts and desires, and to unselfishly give from his most cherished secret treasures, the miracle of the Christmas bells reverberated through him with explosive force!

Charlie watched Joe intently. It was obvious that something terribly important was going on in there.

Joe turned and faced him and tried to speak. His face was white and the words stuck in his throat.

"Are you all right, bud?" Charlie's voice and eyes showed genuine love and concern.

A wave of joy swept over Joe that he couldn't understand, but also couldn't deny. He stared at the pen he had just used as a weapon of vengeance. He dropped it on the cold marble counter top as though it had suddenly heated up and singed his fingers. Then his hands firmly gripped the document of doom he had just signed and slowly and deliberately tore it in half once, then twice, and then crumpled the pieces together into a tight wad which he slam-dunked into a nearby waste basket.

"Joe, what in blazes are you doing?" Charlie's startled voice rang out. "We need that to press charges." He shot a worried glance toward the desk officer, who stared in shocked surprise.

"What's going on here?," Charlie stammered. "Did I miss something I should have caught?"

The color gradually returned to Joe's cheeks. His eyes danced with excitement as he grabbed his old buddy's arm.

"I'm not pressing charges," he said softly.

"You're not pressing. . .what are you talking about?" Charlie yelled. "For the last whole hour you've been railing on that creep back there, and now you say you're. . . ."

"I'M NOT PRESSING CHARGES," Joe's full-volume voice interrupted. His eyes took on an almost wild, determined look. Charlie recoiled in shock. Again he exchanged glances with the desk officer, who was also showing signs of anxiety.

"Wait a minute, Joe! You've gone crazy!" Charlie's voice quivered.

"Charles, old buddy," Joe said with measured deliberation in a voice that increased in pitch and tempo as he spoke. "I've changed my mind. I'm not pressing charges!"

"I don't understand, pal," Charlie responded almost angrily. "You get me out of bed and call me down here in the middle of the night to throw the book at a guy, and then you...."

"I'm not pressing charges, Charlie!" Joe cut him off again. "I'm not pressing charges!" he repeated. "Watch my lips, old buddy." He slowly and emphatically articulated the words, "I'm...not...pressing...charges!"

"Not only that," Joe went on with increasing intensity, "I want you to shift your rusty gears and use all of your legal wizardry to get that handsome young cell-mate of mine out of there. Just don't say anything to him about who did it. If you succeed, he's going to start tomorrow as my newest employee; who knows, maybe even someday my partner! If you fail, you're fired!"

"Somebody get a net!" Charlie gulped. "He's lost it!"

As the worried-looking desk officer reached for the phone Joe reached over and clamped his hand down on the receiver.

"Wait, officer; Charlie, everybody! It's happened. There's no way you can understand this, but it was wonderful. I heard the bells! Just like the Coachman promised! I HEARD THE CHRISTMAS BELLS RINGING IN MY HEART AND I'M NOT PRESSING CHARGES!"

Everyone stared with looks that were, first, akin to panic; But then it began to dawn on them that whatever this strange behavior was, it was not only positive, it was infectious.

"You're right, Joe, I don't understand, but I trust you." Charlie relaxed. He couldn't deny that he'd felt something too. "If you're sure you know what you're saying, and that's what you really want to do, we'll get it set up."

"I've never wanted anything more in my life, old friend."

Then, as if he'd suddenly remembered something he'd forgotten, Joe turned and, with a note of urgency, asked the desk officer if he could use the old battered phone one more time.

"Who are you going to call?" Charlie asked, as if he already knew.

"I've gotta talk to Sue," Joe said with a sense of urgency as he reached for the phone. "I've been ignoring it too long, and it's way past due."

Charlie grinned and nodded. "You won't need a phone," he said as he motioned to the harried female figure that was just then bursting through the huge glass entry doors. With anxious eyes, she glanced around the big room until she found what she'd come for.

"Sue!" Joe yelled in delighted recognition as he turned toward her and took her by both of her out-stretched hands. "What are you doing here?" She looked a little hastily put together, but perhaps even more beautiful than ever before.

"Well, Charlie called and I came," she said. "Where else do you think I'd be? What happened? Are you all right?" Then, as soon as her mind was satisfied that he was all in one piece, the tone of her voice changed. "How is aunt Harriet?" she asked with slightly raised eyebrows.

"I'll explain about all of that later," Joe grinned sheepishly. "Right now, I need to know if you'll marry me."

"What on earth?. . ." Sue started. The color drained from her face as she shot a glance at Charlie, who just cocked his head in a shrugging motion.

"I've loved you forever, but I didn't know how to handle it. But now things are different!" Joe was trying to compress the events of the last twenty-four hours into two minutes and he wasn't sure it was working.

"Of course I'll marry you," Sue suddenly responded. "What girl in her right mind wouldn't? I was beginning to think you'd never ask!" Now the color drained from Joe's cheeks.

A spontaneous cheer went up from the jail staff who'd been gathered to the front by all the commotion. Heaven knows that after their long, tedious night, they were more than ready for a little revelry in their lives.

"You're all witnesses!" Charlie yelled in typical lawyer style.

"We know where you can get a free bed and a good meal for your honeymoon; that is, if you can come by after the holiday rush, Mr. Turner," the jailer with the large ring of keys joked. Laughter rippled through the cavernous old marble foyer. The whole atmosphere had magically changed from the cold stone of civic bureaucracy to the intimate warmth of a loving occasion. Neither the three close friends, nor the jail staff, would ever forget that Christmas, nor the miraculous feeling that wrapped itself around all of them.

Throughout the day, even the jail's beleaguered inmates would benefit, in one way or another, from that radiant love; and have their lives lifted by the peaceful spirit that glowed on and on in that otherwise cold, forlorn place; particularly the good looking young man with the dark curly hair and the old green checkered coat.

A small eight-year-old boy with tear-stained cheeks, who hadn't left his post all night, paced back and forth along the back wall of the marbled foyer. He shot anxious glances, that were mature beyond his years, toward the desk officer who had already told the lad that he had something important to tell him as soon as the three noisy people were gone.

And, in the background from their dwelling place across the street, the Christmas Bells continued their joyous accompaniment of the marvelous experience long into the remainder of the joyous holiday for which they were named.

Epilogue

The good-looking young man with the square jaw and dark, curly hair stepped from the doorway of the precinct jail out onto the sidewalk. A smiling eight-year-old boy clung tightly to one hand as though he wasn't about to let go. His other hand turned the collar of his old green checkered coat up against the frosty morning breeze that stung his tear-stained cheeks.

He inhaled a long, sustaining breath of freedom, and, once again, the emotion of it all flooded over him. There was no question that what he had done was terribly wrong. He would certainly never fall into that kind of trap again. But, in spite of that, the events of the past half-hour had given him a new sense of dignity and worth, and even commitment. He also felt gratitude, and love for an unknown benefactor, and a dozen other strange sensations that he was feeling for the first time in his turbulent young life.

The jailers had reminded him it was Christmas, but what a difference from past Christmases, which had only served as reminders of his sad situation. He had tried so hard to stay strong but, until now, no one had cared to understand how tough things really were.

His mind was reeling from trying to comprehend something that, for him, was incomprehensible. Deep in his pocket, his fingers clutched a wrinkled piece of note paper that the jail's desk officer had handed him as he was released. It contained a simple, incredible hand-written message. Even though he had already read it countless times, he pulled it out and read it once more, just to be sure.

"Charges against you are dropped. Things must have been tougher than anyone will ever know. I hold no grudges. Please accept the watch as a Christmas gift, and the $1,300 as a salary advance for the job you will begin, if you wish, at 8:00 a.m. tomorrow." The note also gave an address that was in a nice area of town, and it was signed "Respectfully, Joe Turner." It had been wrapped around the watch and money he had so forcefully stolen the night before.

To him it was beyond reason, or even belief. Though understandably uneasy and even a little frightened, he couldn't wait to meet this unknown man who had the inner strength and ability to change from the victim of a violent crime to the benefactor of the man who did it. He couldn't imagine the moral character that could make such an act possible. What manner of man could give that much of himself? Whoever it was certainly practiced that Christ-like quality better than anyone he'd ever known.

Of course he would report to his new position first thing in the morning as the note said he should; and whatever the job and whoever the man, he would work harder and give with more devotion than he had ever done before. But for the next several minutes, he was content to just stand with his back to the cold breeze and gaze at the old church across the street and listen, with new insight, to its ringing Christmas Bells.

Now he could earn his living and pay his bills honestly. He could get his loving grandmother the kind of help she needed. He'd just spoken with her over the phone and she would be all right, he just knew it. And he had the money to pay the urgent debt which had caused him to act so foolishly. Once again, those unaccustomed feelings flooded over him. He bent down and hugged the boy and they both let the tears stream un-ashamedly down.

The young man was suddenly aware that someone was standing by him. He hadn't noticed anyone else on the street. He quickly stood and turned to face the quaint smile of an odd, but pleasant-looking old gentleman with a white beard who was dressed in an old-fashioned green long-tailed coat. He wore white spats over spit-shined boots and a tall beaver hat with a sprig of holly tucked in the band.

"Are you all right, my friends?" the old man asked. "Is there anything I can do to help?"

"Sir, we've never been better," the young man replied politely. "But we do appreciate your concern. It's just that I'll bet we've heard those old bells a thousand times, but somehow they've never touched our souls the way they have today. What a joyous sound!

"Merry Christmas to you sir, and thank you for your kindness," the young man smiled.

The old gent's black-gloved fingers just barely touched the brim of his tall hat in a sort of salute as he winked a tear-glistened eye; and in a manner that was strangely knowing he said, "And the merriest of Christmases to you, good lads."

The quaint smile broadened as the boy tugged his big brother downward and softly spoke something into his ear. Then, bidding the old man farewell, they set out hand-in-hand to find a Christmas present for a certain little grandmother who waited at home. . .and that was just the beginning!